A BAD CASE OF STRIPES

DAVID SHANNON

SCHOLASTIC INC.
New York Toronto London Auckland Sydney
Mexico City New Delhi Hong Kong Buenos Aires

To my wife, Heidi;
and to my friend and teacher,
Philip Hays, a.k.a. "Uncle Legend"

This book was originally published in hardcover by the Blue Sky Press in 1998.

ISBN-13: 978-0-439-59838-5
ISBN-10: 0-439-59838-9

25 24 23   13 14 15 16/0

Printed in the U.S.A   40
First Bookshelf Edition, June 2004

amilla Cream loved lima beans. But she never ate them. All of her friends hated lima beans, and she wanted to fit in. Camilla was always worried about what other people thought of her.

Today she was fretting even more than usual. It was the first day of school, and she couldn't decide what to wear. There were so many people to impress! She tried on forty-two outfits, but none seemed quite right. She put on a pretty red dress and looked in the mirror. Then she screamed.

Her mother ran into the room, and she screamed, too. "Oh my heavens!" she cried. "You're completely covered with stripes!"

This was certainly true. Camilla was striped from head to toe. She looked like a rainbow.

Mrs. Cream felt Camilla's forehead. "Do you feel all right?" she asked.

"I feel fine," Camilla answered, "but just look at me!"

"You get back in bed this instant," her mother ordered. "You're not going to school today."

Camilla was relieved. She didn't want to miss the first day of school, but she was afraid of what the other kids would say. And she had no idea what to wear with those crazy stripes.

That afternoon, Dr. Bumble came to examine Camilla. "Most extraordinary!" he exclaimed. "I've never seen anything like it. Are you having any coughing, sneezing, runny nose, aches, pains, chills, hot flashes, dizziness, drowsiness, shortness of breath, or uncontrollable twitching?"

"No," Camilla told him. "I feel fine."

"Well then," Dr. Bumble said, turning to Mrs. Cream, "I don't see any reason why she shouldn't go to school tomorrow. Here's some ointment that should help clear up those stripes in a few days. If it doesn't, you know where to reach me." And off he went.

The next day was a disaster. Everyone at school laughed at Camilla. They called her "Camilla Crayon" and "Night of the Living Lollipop." She tried her best to act as if everything were normal, but when the class said the Pledge of Allegiance, her stripes turned red, white, and blue, and she broke out in stars!

The other kids thought this was great. One yelled out, "Let's see some purple polka dots!" Sure enough, Camilla turned all purple polka-dotty. Someone else shouted, "Checkerboard!" and a pattern of squares covered her skin. Soon everyone was calling out different shapes and colors, and poor Camilla was changing faster than you can change channels on a T.V.

That night, Mr. Harms, the school principal, called. "I'm sorry, Mrs. Cream," he said. "I'm going to have to ask you to keep Camilla home from school. She's just too much of a distraction, and I've been getting calls from the other parents. They're afraid those stripes may be contagious."

Camilla was so embarrassed. She couldn't believe that two days ago everyone liked her. Now, nobody wanted to be in the same room with her.

Her father tried to make her feel better. "Is there anything I can get you, sweetheart?" he asked.

"No, thank you," sighed Camilla. What she really wanted was a nice plate of lima beans, but she had been laughed at enough for one day.

"Hmm, well, yes, I see," Dr. Bumble mumbled when Mr. Cream phoned the next day. "I think I'd better bring in the Specialists. We'll be right over."

About an hour later, Dr. Bumble arrived with four people in long white coats. He introduced them to the Creams. "This is Dr. Grop, Dr. Sponge, Dr. Cricket, and Dr. Young."

Then the Specialists went to work on Camilla. They squeezed and jabbed, tapped and tested. It was very uncomfortable.

"Well, it's not the mumps," concluded Dr. Grop.

"Or the measles," said Dr. Sponge.

"Definitely not chicken pox," put in Dr. Cricket.

"Or sunburn," said Dr. Young.

"Try these," said the Specialists. They each handed her a bottle filled with different colored pills.

"Take one of each before bed," said Dr. Grop.

Then they filed out the front door, followed by Dr. Bumble.

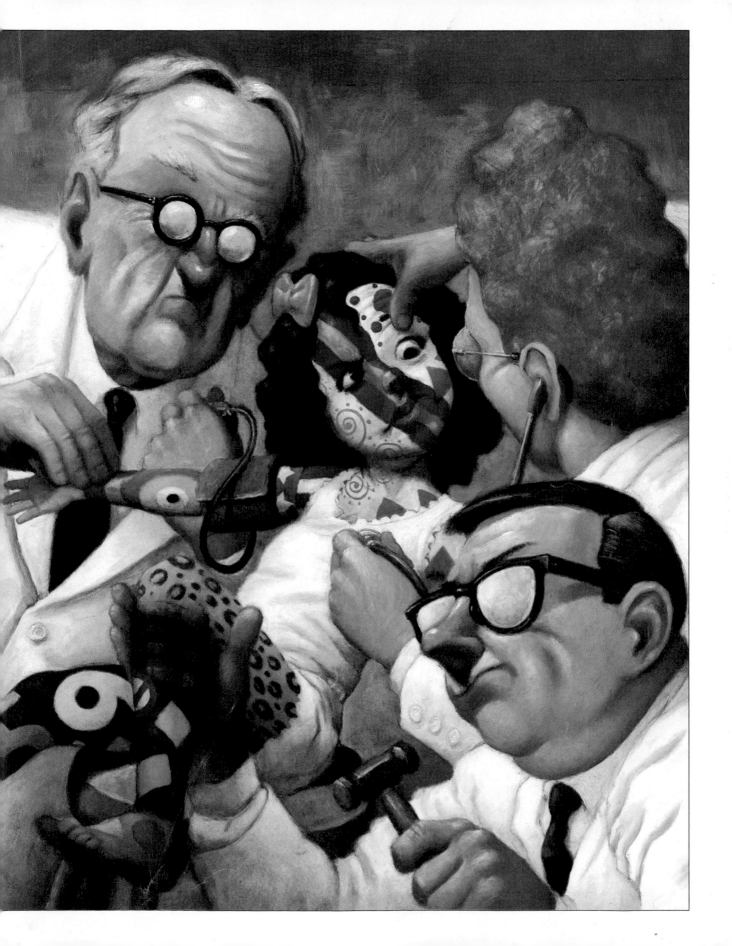

That night, Camilla took her medicine. It was awful. When she woke up the next morning, she did feel different, but when she got dressed, her clothes didn't fit right. She looked in the mirror, and there, staring back at her, was a giant, multi-colored pill with her face on it.

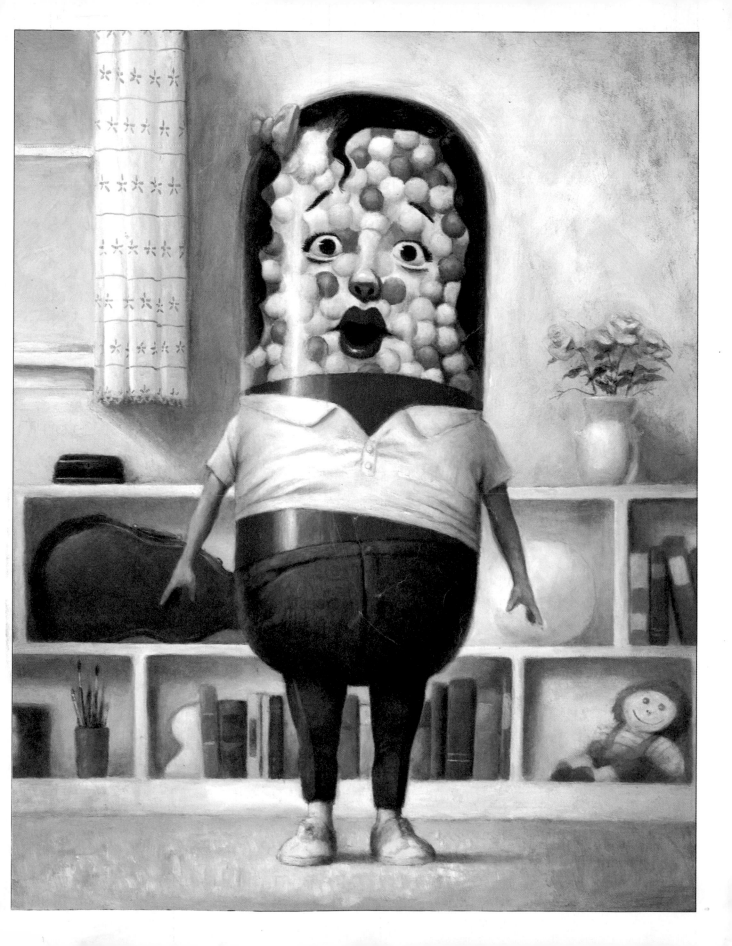

Dr. Bumble rushed over as soon as Mrs. Cream called. But this time, instead of the Specialists, he brought the Experts.

Dr. Gourd and Mr. Mellon were the finest scientific minds in the land. Once again, Camilla was poked and prodded, looked at and listened to. The Experts wrote down lots of numbers. Then they huddled together and whispered.

Dr. Gourd finally spoke. "It might be a virus," he announced with authority. Suddenly, fuzzy little virus balls appeared all over Camilla.

"Or possibly some form of bacteria," said Mr. Mellon. Out popped squiggly little bacteria tails.

"Or it could be a fungus," added Dr. Gourd. Instantly, Camilla was covered with different colored fungus blotches.

The Experts looked at Camilla, then at each other. "We need to go over these numbers again back at the lab," Dr. Gourd explained. "We'll call you when we know something." But the Experts didn't have a clue, much less a cure.

By now, the T.V. news had found out about Camilla. Reporters from every channel were outside her house, telling the story of "The Bizarre Case of the Incredible Changing Kid."

Soon a huge crowd was camped out on the front lawn.

The Creams were swamped with all kinds of remedies from psychologists, allergists, herbalists, nutritionists, psychics, an old medicine man, a guru, and even a veterinarian. Each so-called cure only added to poor Camilla's strange appearance until it was hard to even recognize her. She sprouted roots and berries and crystals and feathers and a long furry tail. But nothing worked.

One day, a woman who called herself an Environmental Therapist claimed she could cure Camilla. "Close your eyes," she said. "Breathe deeply, and become one with your room."

"I wish you hadn't said that," Camilla groaned. Slowly, she started to melt into the walls of her room. Her bed became her mouth, her nose was a dresser, and two paintings were her eyes. The therapist screamed and ran from the house.

"What are we going to do?" cried Mrs. Cream. "It just keeps getting worse and worse!" She began to sob.

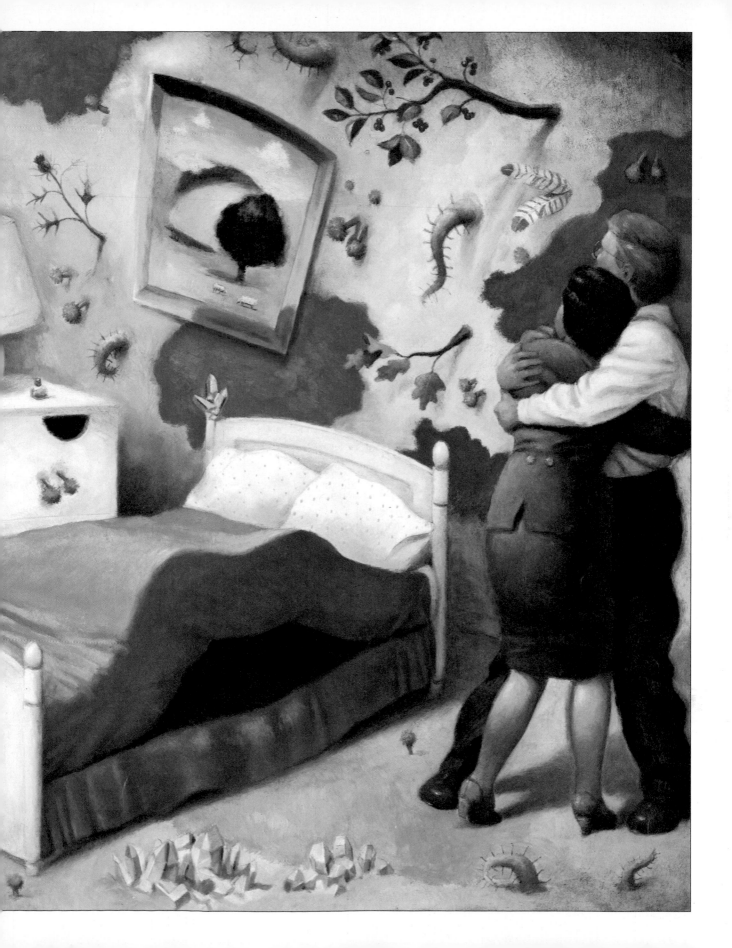

At that moment, Mr. Cream heard a quiet little knock at the front door. He opened it, and there stood an old woman who was just as plump and sweet as a strawberry.

"Excuse me," she said brightly. "But I think I can help."

She went into Camilla's room and looked around. "My goodness," she said with a shake of her head. "What we have here is a *bad* case of stripes. One of the worst I've ever seen!" She pulled a container of small green beans from her bag. "Here," she said. "These might do the trick."

"Are those magic beans?" asked Mrs. Cream.

"Oh my, no," replied the kind old woman. "There's no such thing. These are just plain old lima beans. I'll bet you'd like some, wouldn't you?" she asked Camilla.

Camilla wanted a big, heaping plateful of lima beans more than just about anything, but she was still afraid to admit it.

"Yuck!" she said. "No one likes lima beans, especially me!"

"Oh, dear," the old woman said sadly. "I guess I was wrong about you." She put the beans back in her bag and started toward the door.

Camilla watched the old woman walk away. Those beans would taste *so* good. And being laughed at for eating them was nothing, compared to what she'd been going through. She finally couldn't stand it.

"Wait!" she cried. "The truth is . . . I really love lima beans."

"I thought so," the old woman said with a smile. She took a handful of beans and popped them into Camilla's mouth.

"Mmmm," said Camilla.

Suddenly the branches, feathers, and squiggly tails began to disappear. Then the whole room swirled around. When it stopped, there stood Camilla, and everything was back to normal.

"I'm cured!" she shouted.

"Yes," said the old woman. "I knew the real you was in there somewhere." She patted Camilla on the head. Then she went outside and vanished into the crowd.

Afterward, Camilla wasn't quite the same. Some of the kids at school said she was weird, but she didn't care a bit. She ate all the lima beans she wanted, and she never had even a touch of stripes again.